The STORY KEEPERS

Episode 6

Starlight Escape

Brian Brown and Andrew Melrose

CASSELL

KU-201-469

Cassell
Wellington House, 125 Strand,
London WC2R 0BB

© Brian Brown and
Andrew Melrose, 1997

**Videos distributed by
S. P. Trust**
Triangle Business Park,
Wendover Road, Stoke
Mandeville, Nr. Aylesbury,
Bucks HP22 5BL
Tel. 01296 614430
Fax. 01296 614450

Designed by
Tony Cantale Graphics

All rights reserved.
No part of this publication
may be reproduced or
transmitted in any form
or by any means, electronic
or mechanical including
photocopying, recording or
any information storage or
retrieval system, withour prior
written permission in writing
from the publishers.

First published 1997

**British Library Cataloguing-
in-Publication Data**
A catalogue record for this
book is available from the
British Library.

ISBN 0-304-33665-3

Printed in Spain by
Graficas Reunidas

Long ago, in the city of Rome,
there lived a mighty ruler.
His name was Nero.
He thought he was a god,
but the Christians knew he wasn't.
So Nero hated them.

One day there was a great fire.
Nero said the Christians started it,
and he sent his cruel soldiers after them.

Marcus, Justin and Anna
lost their parents during the fire.
Ben the baker and his wife, Helena,
took them into their home.
There, in a time of great danger,
they told the children stories about Jesus.

This book is about the adventures
of the Storykeepers.

The sky was clear and bright.
An old man named Milo was taking
Ben and the gang to a secret meeting
in the town of Ostia.
Zak was worried. What if the guards
saw them?

Suddenly, horsemen appeared and began to chase them.

"Hold on, everyone!" Milo cried. He cracked his whip and the horses took off running.

"Are you trying to get us killed?" Zak yelled.

Milo veered to the left. The guards went to the right.

"Lost them!" said Milo.

But they had broken a wheel.

"We'll never get to Ostia now," Zak said.

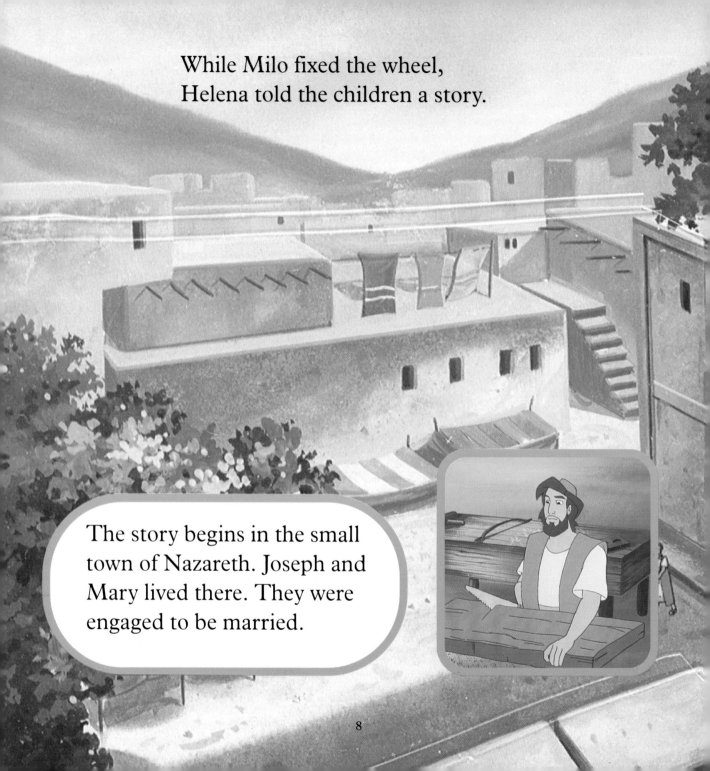

While Milo fixed the wheel,
Helena told the children a story.

The story begins in the small town of Nazareth. Joseph and Mary lived there. They were engaged to be married.

8

One day Mary had a message from God.
"God is pleased with you. You will have a son
and will call him Jesus. He will be great and will
be called the Son of God."

"I will do whatever God wants," Mary said. "Let it happen to me as you have said."

Not far away, shepherds were guarding their sheep.
Suddenly they saw a great light and heard an angel telling them:
"Good news! Your Savior has been born."

The sky was full of angels singing, "Glory to God in heaven, and peace to all people on earth."
The shepherds went to see Jesus and worshiped him.

"Do you know why I like the story of Jesus' birth?" Helena asked. "Because ordinary shepherds were the first to see Jesus."

"I'll go and see why Milo is taking so long,"
said Zak.

He asked Milo a question, but Milo didn't answer.

"This old coot can't hear a thing," Zak scoffed.

"Watch it, sonny," Milo said. "It's a long walk to
Ostia."

Zak blushed.

Soon they were back in the wagon, rattling down
a rough riverbed.
"Whoever heard of driving down a riverbed?"
Zak grumbled.
"Well, one thing's for sure," said Ben. "Nero's
guards will never spot us down here."

At last they stopped
outside a dark inn.
"I'll be right back,"
said Milo.
Zak stopped him.
"Wait! Where are you going?"
"To find out where your meeting is," Milo snapped.

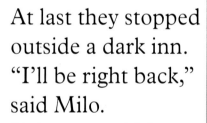

"I don't trust him," Zak grumbled to Ben.
"Calm down," Ben said. "Milo knows what he is doing."

Ben and the children waited,
shivering in the dark.
Suddenly they saw a shooting
star in the sky. So Ben told
the children another story
about some men who
followed a very special star
to Jerusalem.

"They knew that the star meant a king had been born," said Ben. "So they went to the palace of King Herod, a wicked man."

"We have come to worship the child who was born to be king of the Jews," they said to King Herod. "Do you know where we may find him?" Herod was worried. He didn't want someone else to be king.

King Herod sent the visitors to Bethlehem.
"When you find him, come back and tell me where he is," he said.

They found the house where the child was. He was staying there with his parents, Mary and Joseph.

They gave him gifts.
Gold fit for a king, sweet-smelling
incense, and myrrh.

Not long after, the magi left for their own country. They did not go back to Herod. The king was angry, and he was determined to get rid of the child.

"Search the city of Bethlehem. Kill every boy under the age of two," he ordered his soldiers.

That very night an angel appeared to Joseph in a dream and warned him. He, Mary, and Jesus escaped to Egypt.

"King Herod sounds even worse than Emperor Nero!" said Cyrus.

"I like those stories," said Marcus.

"So do I," said a deep voice behind them.

Everyone jumped with fright.

It was a Roman soldier!

Ben recognized the big man.
"This is an old friend," he said.
"Yes, he's a Roman guard. But
he is a Christian too."

Everyone thanked Milo for his help.
Then Zak said, "I'm sorry, Milo, for not
trusting you."
Milo replied, "Ah, you were just looking out
for your friends."
"Yes, but I went too far," Zak admitted.
"A trip like that makes everyone jittery," Milo
said. "Why, a long time ago I took a young
couple to Egypt. They were called Joseph
and Mary, and they had a baby called Jesus.
I wonder what happened to them?"

Milo went off, still talking with himself.
And Zak stood watching as the horse and
wagon disappeared into the night.

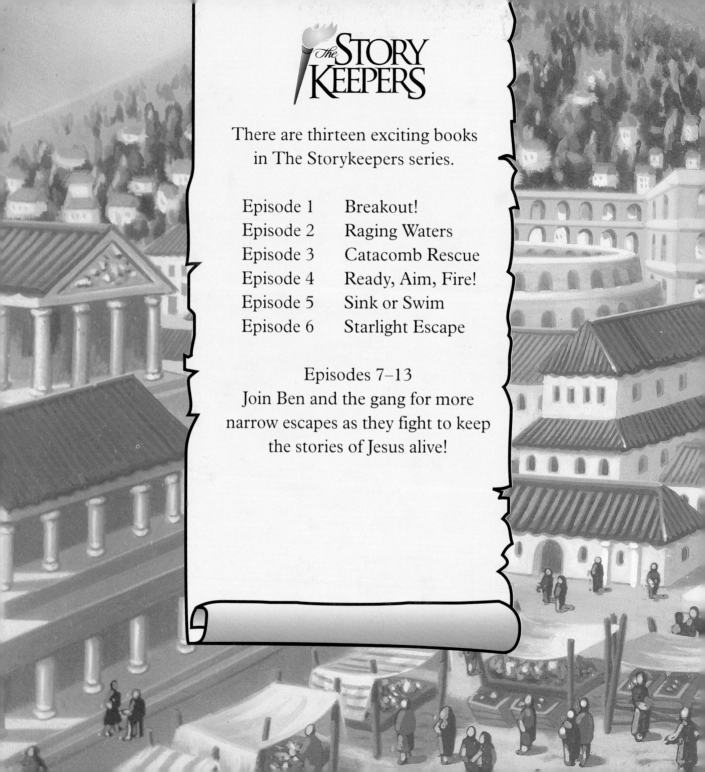

THE STORY KEEPERS

There are thirteen exciting books
in The Storykeepers series.

Episode 1   Breakout!
Episode 2   Raging Waters
Episode 3   Catacomb Rescue
Episode 4   Ready, Aim, Fire!
Episode 5   Sink or Swim
Episode 6   Starlight Escape

Episodes 7–13
Join Ben and the gang for more
narrow escapes as they fight to keep
the stories of Jesus alive!